To Cameron, my muse.
I love you more than chocolate ice cream.

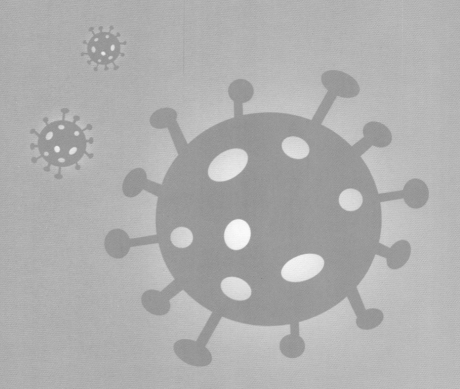

www.mascotbooks.com

NOT NICE, VIRUS!

For more information, please contact:
Mascot Books
620 Herndon Parkway, Suite 320
Herndon, VA 20170
info@mascotbooks.com

Library of Congress Control Number: 2020917290

CPSIA Code: PRT1120A
ISBN-13: 978-1-64543-752-9

Printed in the United States

NOT NICE, VIRUS!

Jordan Morrison

Illustrated by Rachel Novel

There was once a virus that came so fast and quick,

and just like that, the whole world closed so no one would get sick.

The virus makes me angry and sometimes even sad,
because I cannot do things like I always had.

Oh, how I wish I could swim in the neighborhood pool;

don't tell my mom and dad, but I even miss going to school!

Virus, you are taking way too long to go away.
Don't you know all I want to do is to go outside and play?

Not NICE, virus! I yell, I scream, and I pout,
but no matter what I do, the virus will not get OUT!

Can't they take a big old sponge and wash it all away?

But germs are worse than crayon marks,
and it feels like they are here to stay.

Doctors everywhere are working so hard to find a cure.
Soon the world will open up again, of this I am sure.

No more grown-ups in masks unless its Halloween!
And we can all give kisses and hugs with no distance in between.

When the virus goes away,
all the world can laugh and play.

It makes me think as I grow,
There's so much more I want to know.

Germs that are so tiny yet so strong
made so many, many things go so very wrong.

We are bigger, stronger too.

We will make our world anew.

A better world it will be,
a better world for **YOU** and **ME!**

Jordan Morrison

is a mom, wife, and human resources professional—
all of which makes her an exceptional problem
solver. Jordan has always been an avid reader,
and she recently discovered her love for writing.
When the COVID-19 pandemic struck, she found
herself trying to explain a complex new world in
a way that her three-year-old daughter Cameron
could understand. *Not Nice, Virus!* was inspired
by Cameron's inquiries and Jordan's desire to help
other parents with these tough but necessary
conversations around life during the pandemic.